RED HERRINGS

Other Teenage Mutant Ninja Turtle books available in Yearling Books:

RED HERRINGS

D A V E   M O R R I S

Illustrated by Phil Jacobs

A YEARLING BOOK

Published by
Dell Publishing
a division of
Bantam Doubleday Dell Publishing Group, Inc.
666 Fifth Avenue
New York, New York 10103

This work was first published in Great Britain by Yearling books,
Transworld Publishers Ltd.

ISBN: 0-440-40390-1

Printed in the United States of America

June 1990

10 9 8 7 6 5 4 3 2 1

OPM

HEROES IN A HALF SHELL

Fourteen years ago a group of four ordinary turtles that had dropped into the storm drains beneath New York were found by Splinter, a master of the skill of ninjutsu, the ancient Japanese art of stealth and espionage.

Then . . . a leakage of radioactive goo exposed Splinter and his pets to mutating chemicals. Splinter turned into a giant talking rat, while the turtles became the Teenage Mutant Ninja Turtles—his wacky, wisecracking, crime-fighting ninja pupils.

With their human friend, April O'Neil, ace reporter on the Channel 6 TV News, the Turtles fight for what's right and foil the nefarious schemes of the Shredder, Splinter's evil renegade student.

Meet Leonardo, the coolly efficient sword-swinging team leader. Meet Donatello, the expert when it comes to machines; his swishing quarterstaff lays out his foes like bowling pins. Meet Raphael, the prankster, whose wry humor sees the team through perilous situations while his twin daggers send enemies fleeing in panic. And meet Michaelangelo, who's a master of the flying kick and the karate punch and is prepared to use them on anyone who gets between him and a pizza!

"Hey, you guys," said Michaelangelo one morning, "April's on TV."

They all crowded around to see their friend, April O'Neil, standing on the deck of a ship. She was trying not to shiver inside a bright orange sou'wester. "Wherever she is, it looks pretty wet," said Raphael before everybody shushed him.

"This is April O'Neil for Channel 6 News," she was saying, "coming to you by satellite linkup from aboard the survey ship *Masefield* in the mid-Atlantic. Cameras lowered to the seabed yesterday revealed the ruins of a sunken city. I have with me Dr. Rachel Gascoigne, in charge of the survey team. Dr. Gascoigne, can you answer the question on everybody's lips: Have you found Atlantis?"

She held the microphone over toward a short, plump middle-aged woman who looked very excited. "Well, it's too early to be sure," replied Dr. Gascoigne, "but it is starting to look as though the Atlantis legend might be true. Not only that— the probe camera showed signs of what looked like machinery down on the seabed. We'll be lowering a magnetic grabber later to bring some of these machines up for closer inspection. If they confirm what we think from the camera pictures, it may prove that Atlantis had a highly advanced technology. Considering it must have sunk thousands of years ago, this is almost incredible."

"And there you have it," said April, turning back to the TV camera. "Have the ruins of Atlantis been discovered? And did the Atlanteans really have advanced technology? We hope to have the answers for you over the next few days— here on Channel 6 News."

"Wow!" said Donatello, switching off the TV. "How about that, dudes? Don't you envy April, being right on the spot in the middle of a discovery like that?"

"Getting totally soaked and seasick?" said Raphael. "No, thanks!"

Donatello threw up his arms in amazement. "Raph, you got no sense of adventure. According to some Greek guy by the name of Plato, Atlantis was this island civilization that sank below the sea in 9600 B.C. It's the find of the century, dude!"

Master Splinter came out of his room, blearily tying the cord of his bathrobe.

He was always half-asleep first thing in the morning until he'd had a cup of hot green tea. "What's all this commotion out here?" he said with a yawn. He walked over to the kitchen table and surveyed the bits of half-chewed toast and chunks of peanut butter that the Turtles always left behind them after breakfast. "Michaelangelo," he said, "what have I told you about leaving the lid off the marmalade?"

"But, master," protested Michaelangelo, "I got distracted. April was on the TV news. She's on some ship that's discovered a sunken city that—"

"Distracted?" said Splinter, raising a bristly eyebrow. "A ninja must never be distracted, my lad. Now, you should have all started your workout and combat practice ten minutes ago. Snap to it!"

"But, Master Splinter—" piped up Michaelangelo again. He got a clip on the ear for his trouble. Or rather, he would have, if turtles had ears!

♦

April shivered inside her sou'wester. If she could have heard the conversation between Donatello and Raphael, she probably would have agreed with Raph. A great news story was one thing, but was it worth getting seasick and drenched to the skin over? Since the survey ship was at the same latitude as Florida and Madeira, she had thought it would be quite warm. Anticipating the chance for a spot of sunbathing on deck, she'd even packed her swimsuit. In fact it usually would be warmer out here in mid-ocean than inland, but at the moment an unseasonably cold wind was blowing down out of the north, bringing heavy rain and a swell on the sea that made the ship rock constantly. April imagined that she looked just about as sick as she felt, and hadn't dared eat all day.

She was watching the *Masefield*'s

magnetic grabber being winched down to the seabed. It had already brought up a number of metal fragments, which were now arranged in neat rows on the deck. They were badly rusted, of course, but it was still possible to tell that they had come from some sort of machine.

Dr. Gascoigne came up to the rail beside her. Being a good reporter, April forgot about being sick long enough to ask a few questions. "It seems pretty amazing that these devices haven't rusted away entirely. Surely they can't really have been down there since Atlantis sank? Wasn't that supposed to be ten thousand years ago?"

Dr. Gascoigne shrugged. "Plato put it at nearly twelve thousand, but history was a bit more vague in his day. Most archaeologists—those that believe in Atlantis, I mean—would probably say it was about the same time as the empire of Crete, the place that gave us the story of the Minotaur. That makes it a lot more recent. Say it sank in 2000 B.C., then. Even so, the devices we're dredging up must be made of some very special alloy, since ordinary iron and steel would have rusted completely. We won't know for sure until I can run some lab tests."

"What about the ruins themselves?" said April. "They're made of stone, aren't they, so you won't be able to use the magnetic grabber."

"Oh, we don't want to shift them just yet," said Dr. Gascoigne. "We'll want to do that eventually, but at the moment it would be like breaking up a jigsaw before you've got a good look at the picture. We'll need to send down a minisub and take photos from every angle—that way once we finally bring the masonry up and get it back to shore, we've got a reasonable chance of fitting it back together again."

"When will that be?" asked April.

"Oh, not for months. I hope you'll come back to cover the story."

Only if the weather isn't so rough, thought April, stifling a sudden wave of nausea as the ship lurched. Just then, though, the magnetic grabber started to be raised back up by the winch. Curious to see what it would bring up, April forgot all about feeling unwell. She was fascinated to see what new kind of artifact would be revealed.

There was silence from everyone on deck for several minutes as the heavy chain was slowly cranked up. "Whatever it is, it's heavy," said the foreman in charge of the winch mechanism, after a while. Then the magnetic grabber was lifted clear of the water, and they all gasped at the sight of what it had brought up.

For the object, rusted and covered in seaweed though it was, was clearly recognizable as the barrel of a large cannon.

April went on TV again that evening. "There've been exciting new developments during the day," she told millions of viewers. "It now looks as though the Atlanteans were just as advanced in their technology as we are today. The latest objects brought up by the *Masefield*'s grabber include a cannon as large as the ones mounted on modern gunboats. Did they have even more sophisticated weapons? And was it the misuse of those weapons that caused Atlantis to sink? There may be lessons here that we can learn; if Atlantis sank because of careless or greedy use of technology, maybe that has parallels with the modern environment. More as it occurs, from Channel 6 News."

◆

In a secret hideout two strange creatures were watching the broadcast. Both were half-man, half-animal. Bebop, who resembled a wild pig, stared at the screen and sighed. "Duh, isn't she beautiful, dat April. Do yuh t'ink she's got a boyfriend?"

His friend, Rocksteady the rhino, was about equally slow-witted. "Well, I dunno. Anyway, she ain't gonna look twice at youse."

"Naw . . ." said Bebop. He wiped away a tear and blew his nose. It sounded like a bicycle horn.

"Anyways, hadn't we better tell da Shredder about dese weapons? He might want ta go an' steal a few."

Bebop cheered up considerably when he heard that. "Yeah, that'd be a laugh," he said with a chuckle. "I like ta steal t'ings."

"It's heartening," said a voice from behind them, "to find that even a dumb animal can get some pleasure out of life."

Bebop and Rocksteady jumped to their feet and saluted.

"Mista Shredder!" said Bebop. "We gotta tell yuh somet'ing."

"About dese weapons an' stuff out in da sea," added Rocksteady.

The Shredder tapped his metal face-

mask impatiently. "It's a good thing I don't rely on you two cretins for all my information," he said with a snarl. "Fortunately my computers are programmed to lock in on all international news broadcasts, so I already have everything planned. Get into your wetsuits."

"Aww, we ain't takin' the sub, are we?" said Bebop. "I hate goin' underwater."

The Shredder glared at him. "How else do you expect us to get those weapons, you moron? Take a yacht and fishing lines and try to hook them up?"

"Hey, dat's an idea!" said Rocksteady.

"Yes, it's a dumb one! It's the kind of idea you two misfits would have. Now, go and get the sub ready." His two henchmen turned away. As they left the room, the Shredder called after them: "And make sure the torpedo warheads are armed. I don't want those weapons falling into anybody's hands but mine. If that means destroying the survey ship, that's just too bad."

"Yuk, yuk!" said Bebop, rubbing his hands gleefully as he and Rocksteady headed for the submarine bay. "Maybe I'll enjoy dis trip after all. I love blowing t'ings up even more than I like stealing dem!"

Several days later Splinter was putting
our heroes through their paces in their
gym down in the storm drains beneath
New York. Leonardo was practicing with
his favorite sword, parrying thrusts that
Raphael was making with his pronged
sai-daggers. Meanwhile Donatello swung
his quarterstaff around in great sweep-
ing arcs so as to keep Michaelangelo on

his toes—or rather, off his toes, since the object of the exercise was to see how deftly he could leap to avoid getting hit.

"You are enthusiastic and strong, my sons," Splinter was saying, "but the true art of the ninja also requires—"

He was abruptly interrupted by the bleep of their intercom. April was trying to contact them via the personal radio the Turtles had given her. Splinter went to the intercom and flicked a switch. April's face appeared fuzzily on a small video screen set into the wall just above it.

"I recognize those whiskers," said April. "Master Splinter, there are some odd things going on out here. And stuff's been turning up missing. I think you should send the guys to investigate."

"One thing at a time, please, April," said Splinter, his placid voice calming her obvious overexcitement.

Behind him the Turtles were crowding around, pushing past each other for a chance to speak. "What's been missing?" said Donatello. "Which odd things?" said Leonardo. "How can we help?" said Raphael. "We saw you on TV the other night!" said Michaelangelo.

Splinter looked over his shoulder and glared. "Did I not just say, one thing at a time? Now, April, please explain exactly what the trouble is."

"Okay. You probably saw the magnetic grabber on my news report. Dr. Gascoigne's been using it to bring up the metal objects scattered around the ruins of Atlantis. The first few things came up fine, but after getting the cannon, we ran into problems. Somehow things have been disappearing between the time that the grabber locates them on the seabed and the time it takes to winch it up."

Donatello was the expert on gadgets. "It could just be some kind of electrical fault," he suggested.

"I thought of that too," said April. "The grabber's a big electromagnet that runs off the *Masefield*'s generators, so a power cut would deactivate it, but Dr. Gascoigne said that any fault in the wiring would also have affected other instruments aboard ship."

"What about sharks swallowing the items straight off the grabber?" said Leonardo. "They're not too bright, and anything dangling in front of them might look as tempting as a worm on a hook."

"Or whales?" chipped in Michaelangelo.

"The grabber has quite a pull," said April. "I doubt if a shark could tug something off it. Also, some of these items are really big—whales only eat tiny plankton, so that's out. No, I'm beginning to smell a rat."

Splinter raised an eyebrow at this remark, but said nothing. Then, before April could go on, the video picture crackled and was gone. Donatello twisted the radio dial, but all he could get was a hiss of static. "Someone's jamming the broadcast!" he said. "But who—?"

Splinter stroked his whiskers, eyes narrowed in thought. "I have a nasty suspicion about that, my pupils. April is right—you must go out there to investigate."

"Great!" said Michaelangelo as they headed toward the drain tunnels. "I'm going on a seafood diet, dudes."

Raphael looked aghast at him. "A *seafood* diet?"

"Yeah—if I see food, I'm going to eat it! Who's for a stopover at the pizza parlor on our way to the docks?"

◆

April was fast asleep when a Klaxon sounded, jerking her instantly awake. She was out of her room almost before she knew what was going on, running toward the bridge. At the end of the corridor she ran straight into a burly sailor. It was like colliding with a statue, and April staggered back, dazed.

The sailor reached out an arm to steady her. "Whoops," he said. "Sorry, miss, but you ought to look where you're going in future."

April ignored the reprimand—a reporter who stops to think ahead is never going to get a scoop. "What's that siren?" she asked.

The sailor started to head off toward the bridge. "Battle stations," he called back over his shoulder. "It's very serious. You should stay out of the way."

"Battle stations?" said April, following him. "I thought the *Masefield* didn't have any weapons—she's just a survey ship."

"Yeah." The sailor nodded. "That's why it's serious!"

When they reached the bridge, April found everyone clustered around the sonar screen. She slid in beside Dr. Gascoigne and saw an ominous green blip approaching the *Masefield*'s position.

The Captain looked up. His face was

set in an expression of steely calm. "Given the speed of that thing, it must be an incoming torpedo. I'd like all non-crew members to leave the bridge immediately. Mr. Silver," he nodded at the first mate, "would you sound the horn to abandon ship, please."

"A torpedo!" said April to Dr. Gascoigne as they were bustled toward the ship's boats. "I have to find my cameraman. We have to get some pictures of this for the six-o'clock news."

Dr. Gascoigne had other concerns. "I'm going to grab some of the smaller artifacts we dredged up from Atlantis," she said. "It'd be awful if they all sank back to the bottom of the ocean after the trouble we've been to."

"You're both crazy!" said one of the other scientists. "In about ninety seconds this ship's going to have a hole in the side big enough to drive a jeep through. I intend to get aboard the life raft as soon as possible."

Suddenly the ship lurched as the helmsman tried to bring her around. If only they could turn in time, the torpedo might just miss them. But it was a desperate maneuver, and it did not look as though it was going to work. The ship could not possibly turn fast enough.

"Hey, LOOK!" A technician was standing at the rail pointing off toward the horizon. Everybody stopped and stared, transfixed at the sight of a white furrow moving straight as an arrow through the water toward the *Masefield*. A sort of moan of dread went up from everyone's lips. "There isn't time to reach the boats," wailed somebody. "We're doomed!"

In the midst of all the panic April was still looking around for her cameraman. Just as she saw and waved to him, she caught a glimpse of something out of the corner of her eyes. Turning, she peered out to sea. Four figures were visible on fast-moving water scooters, racing in toward the torpedo. Four *green* figures.

"Get a zoom lens trained on those guys," she yelled to the cameraman. "I've got a feeling we're going to see some action." She was thinking how this would show the cynics back home—including her boss at Channel 6—that the Turtles really were heroes, not mutant menaces.

◆

Way out at sea the Turtles had spotted the torpedo on their miniature radar. "It's either a torpedo or a shark who hasn't switched to decaffeinated," Raphael said, watching the blip on the screen set between his scooter handlebars. "What are we going to do about it, dudes?"

"I'm going in close," yelled Donatello over the roar of the scooter engines. "You three hang around here to pick up survivors if my plan doesn't work."

"Hey, Don, wait—!" shouted Leonardo. But it was too late: Donatello had already veered off and was now on a direct collision course with the torpedo.

"Oh boy, what's he up to?" gasped Michaelangelo.

Hardly daring to breathe, they watched as Donatello steered his water scooter in beside the torpedo and then leaped across onto the back of it. Driverless, the scooter sped off across the water. Donatello, meanwhile, was having to hang on for dear life as the torpedo carried him inexorably nearer to the *Masefield*. A white spray was gushing back over him and threatened to fling him off the speeding torpedo. Inch by agonizing inch he crawled forward until he was just behind the warhead. He fumbled at his belt, blinded by the spray, and managed to find his screwdriver.

"Don!" screamed April from the ship's rail. "Jump clear!" She had her hands pressed to her mouth in horror, but she had completely forgotten the danger that she and the others were in. All she could

think of now was that when the torpedo exploded, Donatello would be sitting right on top of it!

With the surf chopping past him, Donatello could not hear April's shouts, nor the warnings of his brothers. With gritted teeth, he set to work removing the access panel behind the warhead. He spared the time to glance up. The *Masefield* was still turning about slowly, but the torpedo would definitely hit her. Donatello estimated there were about twenty seconds left before impact. He pulled off the access cover and tore at the wiring inside.

Leonardo gunned his scooter engine, but he could not catch up with the torpedo now. It was skimming along the waves, with Donatello riding on its back like a cowboy on a bucking bronco. "Don," he called hopelessly over the noise of the scooter, "it's too late. You'll only get yourself killed!"

Fifteen seconds to go. Donatello was

a genius at electronics and any other sort of gadgetry. Pulling two wires loose, he twisted them together and adjusted a capacitor. The torpedo gave a violent shudder and began to change course.

On board the *Masefield* the engine ship's company was gathered along the rail. They all held their breath and watched in awe. The only sound was the soft whirr of the TV camera following Donatello's every move.

"Go on, turn, dammit!" snarled Donatello. He gave the capacitor another twist, then wrenched it out and struck the inertial guidance system manually. "There's never a monkey wrench handy when you need one," he said, grunting, to himself.

"It's still going to hit!" gasped Dr. Gascoigne, her voice no more than a choked whisper. Everyone began to step back from the rail—not that that would do any good. The torpedo could blow the whole side off the ship.

Only a few seconds remained. "So much for subtlety!" said Donatello in exasperation. "Hii-YAA!" He slammed his fist down in a powerful karate punch against the casing around the steering gyro. The torpedo tilted violently, flinging him off into the water, then turned to one side and scraped past within inches of the ship. A great cheer went up from everyone on board.

"Wow!" said April. "What a rescue— and we got it all on film!"

There was a thud on the deck behind her. She turned and sighed; the cameraman had fainted.

The Turtles were bringing their scooters in toward the *Masefield,* scouring the water for any sign of Donatello. "He might have hit his head when he jumped," said Michaelangelo nervously.

Just as they were beginning to think of diving for him, Donatello rose to the surface and gave them a thumbs-up. "Glub," he said, spitting out seawater. "Thirsty work, this."

"Hey, dude," said Raphael, "you hitching a lift?"

"Sure," said Donatello, clambering aboard Raphael's scooter, "if you're going my way."

Naturally everybody wanted to thank the Turtles for saving the ship. They were just about mobbed for autographs, and then the Captain invited them to dine with him. It was some time before April got a proper chance to talk to them.

"Master Splinter thinks somebody is stealing these weapons off the magnetic grabber in order to learn the secrets of ancient Atlantis," said Leonardo after April had filled them in on what had been happening.

"Presumably the same somebody that tried to torp the ship," put in Michaelangelo. Despite his full meal at the Captain's table, he was now munching on a pizza he had swiped from the kitchens.

"What about Splinter?" said April. "Since it's so important, he surely should have come too."

"Unlike us, he doesn't like the water," explained Leonardo.

"Yeah," added Raphael, "and anyway you know what they say about rats and sinking ships . . ."

April laughed. "Well, fortunately we haven't sunk yet—thanks to Don. The question is, what's the next step?"

"We're going to have to swim down to the ruins and take a look around," said Leonardo. "There might be some clue down there as to who's snatching the relics off the grabber."

"I don't think the ship has scuba gear to fit you guys," said April as they went out on deck.

"So who needs scuba gear?" said Raphael nonchalantly. "We're turtles; we can breathe underwater. . . . Hey, Don, what're you doing, dude?"

Donatello was a short distance away across the deck, crouched beside a rusted metal cannon—one of the first relics the magnet had brought up. He had a tape measure in his hand. "Hmm, three hundred and eighty-one millimeters. That's exactly fifteen inches," he muttered as the others came over.

"What's that?" said April.

Donatello looked up. "The shells fired by this gun," he said as he put the tape measure away, "would have been just over thirty-eight centimeters wide."

Michaelangelo whistled. "Big!"

Donatello scratched his head. "Ummm . . . But there's something fishy about this. I can't quite put my finger on it right at the moment, though."

"I dare say it'll come to you, Don," said Leonardo briskly. "For now, we're driving down to take a look at the ruins. Better get some lamps."

They each went off to fetch weapons and equipment, regrouping on deck a few minutes later. Donatello had a long coil of rope and a net. "We might want to shift some of the masonry down there," he said.

"Hey, look, you guys!" yelled Michaelangelo. He had arranged a plank over the side of the ship so that it could be used like a diving board. As they turned to watch, he ran to the end of the board, leaped off, did a somersault in midair, and hit the water perfectly.

"Fools rush in . . ." said Raphael drily.

Leonardo got out onto the diving board. "Oh, don't be such a grouch, Raph. It's as good a way as any of getting into the water. Geronimo!" He, too, dived off into the dark blue-gray ocean.

Raphael followed. Just as Donatello

was about to dive after his brothers, he thought of something. "April, I've had an idea that might help flush out our thief. I want you to prepare a special TV broadcast . . ."

Donatello spent a couple of minutes explaining his plan. Then the heads of the other three broke the surface. "Come on, Don!" they called in unison.

"Okay, I'll be right with you," he replied. "You're sure you've got all that, April?" As he nodded, Donatello ran along the board, sprang up on tiptoe, dived down toward the others, and entered the water in a classic bellyflop. Fortunately, that isn't too painful for a turtle.

Under the water everything looked weird. There was a bluish gloom, like twilight, and as they swam deeper, the Turtles had to switch on the lamps they had brought.

"I hope there aren't any sharks," said Raphael. His voice sounded funny in the water.

"Not around here," Donatello assured him. "I checked it out with one of the ship's scientists before we came down."

"Eyes front, guys," said Leonardo. "It looks like we've found Atlantis!"

On the seabed below them their lamps revealed an astonishing sight. Cracked stone pillars littered the floor of the ocean in between the broken walls and gaping porticoes of an ancient sunken city. Seaweed grew over the masonry, slowly swaying in the ocean currents. It was amazing to think that they were looking at things that had been built thousands of years ago.

The lamps cast eerie shadows off the seaweed, but Michaelangelo steeled his nerves and swam right down into a large building. "This might once have been the king's palace," he said, seeing a weathered marble throne inside. "Did Atlantis have kings?"

"No one knows anything about it," said Donatello. "Hey, Mike, don't get out of sight of the rest of us."

Michaelangelo floated over to sit on the throne. "Don, you're such a worry-wart sometimes."

Raphael braced himself between two loose pillars. "Look at this, I'm Samson!" He pushed, and the pillars toppled over, falling with majestic slowness.

"Don't muck about," said Leonardo sharply. "You might bring the whole palace—what's left of it—down around our ears." As he called the others to order, he outlined the plan: "We'll split up, but each of us has to keep one of the others in sight at all times. That way we can scour the ruins a lot quicker."

"What are we looking for, Leo?" asked Michaelangelo. "Weapons and gadgets and things?"

"No. They can bring those up on the magnet, and in any case there don't seem to be any lying around in this part of the ruins."

"Lagan," said Donatello.

Leonardo looked at him. "Say it again, Don?"

"Lagan," said Donatello again. "It's what they call stuff that's left on the seabed."

Leonardo nodded, unimpressed. "Thanks for that little gem of information, bro'. But you aren't looking for widgets, gadgets, lagan, krakens, or anything like that. We're looking for someplace that someone could hide a sub. That torpedo had to come from somewhere!"

They swam into formation and began to drift above the ruins, playing their flashlights this way and that. Whenever a building large enough to hold a submarine was found, one of them dived down to investigate.

"Ignore anywhere with the walls more or less intact," said Leonardo. "It would have to be a place the sub could get in and out of."

Raphael signaled to the others and started to approach a large colonnaded hall. "Check this place out," he called.

"It's as big as a hangar; easily large enough for—YIPES!!"

A forest of tentacles shot out from a crack in the building's roof, seizing Raphael. He reached for his sai-daggers, but had barely drawn one before the tentacles pinned his arms. Slowly a giant octopus hauled itself into view, eyes glaring balefully from above a sharp, poison beak.

"Hang on, Raph!" shouted Michaelangelo, darting in to the attack. He struck two strong karate blows against the nearest tentacle, but the water took most of the momentum out of his strikes. It was just like hitting a huge slab of rubber anyway.

"We need an edge," observed Donatello as he and Leonardo swam over to join the fray. "Brother, can you spare a sword?" Each armed with a katana, they hacked at the tentacles. The octopus loosened its grip enough for Raphael to get one arm free, but when he tried to

stab at its eyes with his sai, it withdrew its body into the building. The tentacles still flailed about, battering the Turtles and trying to snatch away their weapons.

Leonardo tried a handful of shuriken, but it was pointless trying to throw them underwater. They went in all directions for a yard or so and then fell to the seabed. Meanwhile Raphael, still held by a tentacle around his legs, was being pulled relentlessly toward the hole.

"Don't let it bite you, Raph," cried Donatello urgently. "Its beak is poisonous."

Even in deadly peril, Raphael had time for sarcasm. "What do you think— that I'm just playing with it?" he snapped. "I'm trying *not* to let it bite me, for pete's sake!"

Leonardo and Michaelangelo grabbed him and started a tug-of-war with the octopus while Donatello kept chopping at its tentacle with the katana-sword. Unfortunately it was difficult to get the angle right while striking underwater. Another tentacle shot out and snaked around Raphael's waist. "It's no good, guys," he said with a grunt, straining against the octopus's pull. "It's got six more where those two came from." As it wrenched him closer to the hole, he braced his legs against the roof of the building. "Quick, Don, hand me your bo!"

Donatello hastily unstrapped the long staff from his back. "It won't be any use," he protested. "You can't get any force behind the swing down here." Nonetheless he handed it over.

Raphael took off his bandanna, using it to tie one of his sai to the end of the staff. Despite the assistance of the others, his legs were getting tired. If his plan didn't work the first time, he was doomed to be the octopus's next meal. Drawing the staff up like a spear, he took careful aim. "Here's one in the eye for you, chum!" he snarled. And he plunged his makeshift weapon down through the hole in the roof.

There was a chopping sound like someone driving a skewer into a cabbage, then a horrible sucking. Blood and black ink rose from the octopus's lair. Raphael felt the tentacles fall away as the wounded creature fled.

"Whew!" said Michaelangelo. "That was a close shave. Are octopuses usually that unfriendly?"

"They're not usually that *big*," said Donatello, wafting the ink away. "Too bad we didn't get a chance to follow it. I've a feeling it might have led us to an old foe."

That evening, they sat around the TV in April's cabin. "Here's a report I taped earlier today," she said. "It's going out now on Channel 6 News."

They watched the filmed report: "This is April O'Neil aboard the survey ship *Masefield,* bringing you the latest developments on the discovery of Atlantis. The big news is that the Mutant Turtles turned up today in the nick of time to avert a major disaster when the *Masefield* was mysteriously torpedoed. More on that, with film, at eleven. Additionally, scientists report that several small relics have been brought up from the ocean bed, including a device that seems to be some sort of ray gun. Technicians aboard ship have every hope of getting it working again, despite the thousands of years it must have spent lying on the ocean floor. Follow this and other stories at eleven."

"*What* ray gun?" scoffed Raphael. "I haven't heard anything about any ray gun—or about anything being brought up today, for that matter."

"Aha," said April with a smile as she switched off the TV set. "You didn't hear anything because it's not true. It's a hoax. Don's idea. He told me about it just before you all dived down to the ruins."

"Don," said Leonardo. "Can you explain?"

"Think about it, guys," said Donatello. "Suppose you were some big bad thief in a sub. You've been filching cannons and so forth off the electromagnet, but what you really want is something that still works—not a weapon that you're going to have to study for years to find out how to rebuild it. A real honest-to-gosh superweapon. A ray gun. What would you do after seeing that TV report?"

"Nice plan, Don," said Michaelangelo with a cheer. "All we have to do is wait, and the guy who's been stealing those relics is going to come right to us."

Leonardo nodded. "And I don't think we'll have to wait very long. Unless I miss my guess, he'll come aboard tonight. Come on guys—we have to prepare a welcome!"

◆

Midnight had come and gone, and clouds covered the moon, when two figures in frogman outfits hauled themselves out of the water and up the ladder of the *Masefield*. Clambering over the rail, they looked warily around. There was no sign of anybody on deck.

"Right," said one. "Dis is da ship. Now all we gotta do is find dis ray gun."

"Da boss said ta whisper, though, Rocky," whispered the other. He pulled off his scuba mask to reveal a boar's face.

"Oh, yeah. And we gotta tiptoe too."

"Dat's right—an' no unnecessary noise, neider."

"Yep, no blabbin' about nonsense, da boss said."

"He said we were to get right on wid da job, grab da ray gun, an' get back to da sub."

Rocksteady nodded. "Okay, it looks like we both got da plan straight in our heads. We better keep an eye out for the watch. Dere's gotta be a few sailors awake, even at dis time of night."

"Gee, Rocky," said Bebop. "I just realized—I never been up dis late before."

"Sure you did," Rocksteady contradicted him. "What about dat Christmastime we went ta steal da toys from da orphans' home?"

"Oh, yeah. I forgot dat. An' we swiped da Christmas tree outta Rockefeller Center on our way back home. Haw, haw, dat was a laugh."

"What was?" said Rocksteady.

"Dat sound I just made 'cause I thought somet'in was funny."

"Oh, yeah, dat was a laugh all right."

Reminiscing about their revolting lives of petty crime, the two set off toward the companionway that led below deck. They passed no sailors on watch—not because they were particularly stealthy but because Leonardo had already warned the Captain to keep his men out of sight. The Turtles were looking forward to catching their enemy.

Bebop and Rocksteady reached the bottom of the companionway ladder. "Which way now?" whispered Rocksteady.

"It'd be in da labs, I guess. Let's try dis way." Bebop led the way along the passage toward the stern. They had not gone far before they came to a door with a hastily scrawled sign taped to it.

"What does it say, Bebop?"

Bebop stared at it. "Duh . . ." he said at last. "I t'ink it says, *Ray Gun Lab. Thieves Keep Out.*"

Rocksteady clapped him on the shoulder excitedly. "Then dis must be da place! Let's go in, Bop."

Pulling open the door, they stepped inside. It was dark. Bebop flicked the switch, but the light did not come on. "Da dratted bulb must've gone," he said with a sour grunt. "You remember ta bring da flashlight, Rock?"

"Whaddya mean?" said Rocksteady from behind him. "You was da one bringin' da flashlight."

"Why argue, fellas?" said a voice out of the darkness. "After all, you both goofed."

Bebop jumped back, startled, and collided with his friend so that they both went sprawling. "Did ya hear that, Rocky? Dere's someone in here wid us."

"Not some*one*," said another voice. "Some *four*. Turtles, let's see some action!"

Rocksteady scrambled to his feet. "It's da Turtles, Bop," he yelled. "Let's get 'em before dey get us!"

At that moment, just to further complicate matters for the two ruffians, April slammed the door shut behind them. In total darkness the Turtles' ninja training gave them all the advantages. April waited until the shouts and crashes from inside the room had given way to groans, then opened the door. Bebop and Rocksteady were neatly trussed up like Christmas turkeys, with the Turtles standing over them.

"I gotta say it," whimpered Bebop."What a revoltin' development!"

"Dat's da truth," admitted Rock-

steady. "Er—look, youse guys. . . . Maybe we can do a deal?"

"Sure," said Raphael. "You tell us where the stolen weapons are and we might just not throw you to the sharks."

"Da SHARKS!" Rocksteady screeched. "Oh no—I ain't got over *Jaws III* yet!"

Bebop shushed him. "Hey, they're just bluffing. Da Shredder told us dere ain't no sharks around this part of da ocean."

Leonardo leaned down and stared Bebop squarely in the eyes. "So, just as we suspected, the Shredder is behind all this. Where's he hiding out now?"

"He's got a real dinky little sub," said Rocksteady.

"Yeah. We're his crew," boasted Bebop.

Raphael looked down at the sorry pair, his hands on his hips. "Well, I never thought I'd say it, but I pity the Shredder if you're the best henchmen he can find."

Bebop snarled defiantly. "You better

start shakin' in your socks, turtle boys. When da boss gets those Atlantis weapons working, you're gonna be turtle soup—*capiche*?"

Donatello went over to the door and pulled off the taped notice. Underneath, the real sign read: STOREROOM. "Well," he said to the two villains, with a wink to the other Turtles that Bebop and Rocksteady didn't see, "if the Shredder attacks, he'll be making bacon and rhino steaks out of you guys."

"That's right, Don," said Leonardo as he ushered the others out of the storeroom. "I guess these fellas must be so brave that they don't mind dying for their master, though."

Michaelangelo was the last out. He turned as he was closing the door. "Horrible to be tied up and locked in a storeroom when the ship sinks," he said in a stage whisper. "But Bebop and Rocksteady are good soldiers. They're prepared to sacrifice themselves if need be."

"Hey, wait up!" called Bebop nervously.

"Yeah," said Rocksteady. "Don't leave us here widdout a light."

Leonardo pulled the door open again. "Surely you aren't telling me that you're afraid of the dark?"

"It ain't dat!" Bebop replied. "We just don't want to go down to a watery grave if our boss decides ta torp dis ship again."

Donatello smiled at the others. "In that case," he said, "you'd better tell us where we can find him."

"Awright, awright," Rocksteady agreed. "But ya gotta promise not ta say we said so. Da boss can get awful mad."

"He's in a minisub," said Bebop. "Dere's an underwater cave not too far from here. Dat's where da sub's parked. Ya can't miss it, 'cause dere's a statue in da ruins dat points to it. And dat's where he's keeping da weapons he stole."

"Yay!" cried Michaelangelo. "Come on, dudes. Let's go can the Shredder!"

"Say, Bop," murmured Rocksteady after April and the Turtles had left them alone. "Do ya t'ink dat was a good idea, telling dem about da Shredder's sub an' all?"

"Sure," replied Bebop. "We didn't tell dem about da robot shark dat Baxter made for him, after all. It'll chew dem turtles inta tiny pieces. Haw, haw!"

They both sniggered evilly in the darkened storeroom.

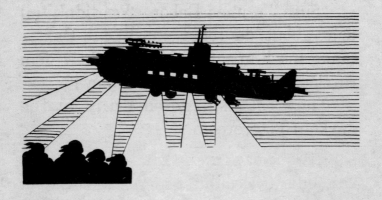

The Turtles waited until dawn before
diving back down to the ruins. April, Dr.
Gascoigne, and several of the *Masefield*'s
officers stood at the rail to wish them
good luck. A cold, gray light filtered
across the water from behind lowering
clouds to the east, and an albatross cir-
cled wearily overhead. April looked at it
and shivered; *I hope that isn't a sign of
bad luck,* she said to herself.

Donatello pointed to a small device, like a radio pager, that each of the Turtles had clipped to their belts. "These little gizmos I cooked up will send out a strong ultrasonic signal," he explained. "It's too high-pitched to hear, but it'll let you track our progress on the ship's sonar."

April shrugged. "I can't see how that's going to do much good, since there's no way for us to speak to you. Even if we saw something dangerous coming at you on the sonar, we couldn't send a warning."

"That isn't the point, April," said Leonardo very seriously. "It's just so you know, should anything happen to us." He turned to the Captain. "And if anything does, you should get the *Masefield* out of the area immediately. The Shredder won't give up till he's got all the sunken weapons."

The Captain nodded and sucked at the pipe that he habitually had clamped between his teeth. "That's commendable bravery, son," he said. "You may be green, but certainly no one could call you yellow. I'll hold on as long as I can for you to get back—but, as you say, my first priority is this ship and everyone aboard her."

"C'mon, guys," said Michaelangelo with a moan. He had already clambered over the rail. "We can't have breakfast until we get this dip over with!" He jumped off and plunged into the sea.

"Last one in is a banana," yelled Raphael, flipping over the side and turning in midair so as to hit the water in a dive. Donatello followed him, using his bo-staff to pole-vault over the rail.

Leonardo grinned. "Looks like you were wrong, Captain. I'm the yellow one after all." He saw the baffled expression on the Captain's face. "Think about it." And with that he dived off into the surging waters.

Treading water, the Turtles allowed themselves to drift slowly down until they were close to the seabed, then switched on their lamps. "Let's go slowly and keep close to the bottom," said Leonardo. "We don't want the Shredder to spot our beams."

"I wonder if he's missed his two stooges yet," said Raphael as they swam across the ruined city.

"He ought to thank us for taking them off his hands," said Donatello, chuckling. "Those guys are too dumb to tie their own bootlaces."

"Shh!" said Leonardo. "Look, up ahead."

Michaelangelo grumbled something under his breath. "Shh, he tells us. How am I supposed to keep my stomach from rumbling when it hasn't been fed yet today?"

They were approaching an imposing statue that rose spectacularly out of a heap of weed-covered masonry. The statue depicted a warrior woman clad in metal armor with a spear in her hand.

Displaced from her pedestal over the millennia, she was leaning at an alarming angle but was held upright by the wedged blocks of stone around the base. Her hand pointed off into the murky gloom ahead.

Donatello swam in for a closer look. "I'm no expert, but this doesn't look to me like the kind of statue that a highly advanced technological society would put up."

"Never mind that," said Raphael. "It's where she's pointing that matters to us."

They set out. Slowly a shadowy shape came into view, looming darkly in the marine haze. As he realized that it was actually moving toward them, Leonardo turned his lamp on it. The light glinted off a polished steel snout, beneath which a gaping mouth was filled with rotating saw-toothed wheels.

"A robot shark!" yelled Michaelangelo.

"Must be Baxter's work," surmised Donatello.

"If no one else is going to say it," screeched Raphael, "then I will: *duck!*"

As they darted aside, the shark shot past them like an undersea missile. Huge propellors churned the water behind it, and it cut through the sea with razor-sharp blades set like fins along its flanks. Leonardo would have been decapitated if he hadn't pulled his head back into his shell at the last instant. "Phew, that was a close call," he said as he popped his head back out. "It's at times like this that I'm glad I'm a turtle."

"At times like this," said Raphael, "I'd personally rather be a sixty-ton battleship. Watch out, everybody, it's turning for another pass."

Hatches opened along either side of the robot's burnished body, and it suddenly sprouted two huge harpoon guns. Barbed points gleamed in the water-filtered lamplight.

"Watch out for those," said Leonardo as the robot started back toward them, though no one needed to be told.

"Here, Leo, you take this," Donatello said, handing his bo to Leonardo.

Leonardo looked puzzled. "I thought we already decided weapons like the bo aren't any use underwater."

"It might make a neat toothpick for Jaws there," explained Donatello. "Once you've done that, try luring it back the way we came. I'm going to set a shark trap!"

Leonardo was more used to giving orders than taking them, but in this case he did not have a better plan. As Donatello swam off, he moved in toward the hurtling robot. With an explosive hiss one of the guns fired and a harpoon came shooting toward him. He managed to twist aside so that it skidded harmlessly off his shell. As the other gun fired, he swung the bo. The harpoon embedded itself in the wooden staff with a thunk.

"Sharp shooting, sharky," said Michaelangelo, "but not sharp enough." He darted in and delivered a powerful blow to the robot's head with a tonfa-club. As it reacted, twisting to try to catch him in its blade-filled jaws, Leonardo swam up and stuck the bo right in its mouth. There was a frenzied grinding of gears as it tried to force its mouth shut. The bo began to crack.

"Quick!" said Leonardo. "We've got to get it to chase us."

"I think we just need to swim off," said Raphael. "It'll take care of the chasing part without any encouragement from us!"

Praying that Donatello was ready, the three set off with the robot in hot pursuit. Glancing back, they could see that the bo was beginning to give under the enormous strain of the robot's jaw motors. At any moment it would snap the bo like a twig.

The statue came in sight, still leaning like the Tower of Pisa above the ruins. Donatello had cast his net and tackle around it and hastily tricked up a pulley weighted by a block of stone. The Turtles swam under the outstretched arm and then, while Leonardo trod water to bait their robot pursuer, the others went down to help Donatello.

"Here it comes," said Donatello. "Heave ho!"

Putting all their weight on the cable, the three Turtles tugged for all they were worth. It did not move an inch.

"Keep trying," grunted Donatello. "We have to get it going against the weight of the masonry. Gravity will do the rest."

"I think what Don's trying to say, Mike," said Raphael, "is Let's put some English on it!"

Finding reserves of strength they had never tapped before, they redoubled their efforts. After a moment the pulley started to turn, paying out the cable an inch at a time. And slowly—painfully slowly—they saw the net go taut around the statue and begin to pull it over.

The robot shark was hurtling at full tilt toward Leonardo. Its nose passed under the statue's arm, moving like a torpedo through the water.

"There isn't time!" gasped Michaelangelo. "Leo—get out of the way!"

Even as he said that, the cable went suddenly slack. They glanced up to see the statue toppling, dredging up great chunks of rubble and clouds of muck and weeds from the ocean floor as it fell. Its arm struck the shark's back, glanced along the polished metal surface, and caught against the propellor casing at the tail. The shark was carried down by the enormous weight of stone, and wound up pinned to the seabed with the statue's arm lying across it. It thrashed about wildly for a few seconds, then Raphael swam over and jammed its propellor with a sai. "Even if it gets out from under the statue, it won't be able to move anywhere," he said.

"Wow, Leo," said Michaelangelo,

breathing a sigh of relief, "you certainly have nerves of steel. I never would've been able to stay right in front of it till the last moment the way you did."

Leonardo opened his eyes. "Is it all over?" he said. "I couldn't bring myself to watch."

◆

Up on board the *Masefield,* April and the others had managed to follow some of the action at least. "They encountered something fast-moving," said the ship's sonar operator as he bent over the screen. "I'd say it was a guided torpedo."

"But they've dealt with it somehow?" asked Dr. Gascoigne, craning over his shoulder for a look.

"It looks that way. It's stopped moving, but there's another incoming blip now. This one is much larger; it looks like a sub."

"The Shredder!" gasped April. "The

guys can't fight an entire submarine. We have to warn them!"

"We don't have any way of doing that, Miss O'Neil," said the Captain solemnly. "All we can do is cross our fingers and hope they get away."

April looked around at everyone on the bridge. "Crossing fingers is not a lot different from twiddling thumbs!" she said sharply. "Well, *I'm* going to do something." She stormed out on deck and marched over to the electromagnet that the scientists had been using to fish for metal fragments. It had a number of gear levers, but she did not have much trouble getting it started and lowering the magnet down into the sea. Now all she could do was hope that her idea would work—and that she wasn't too late already.

◆

"Hey, can you guys hear something?" asked Donatello, cupping his ear.

Leonardo nodded. "Sounds like the engines of a sub. The Shredder must have seen us coming."

Michaelangelo glanced at the broken robot shark. "Maybe his little pet had a built-in camera," he said.

Just then Raphael spotted something. He pointed off into the murky waters. "Heads up, fellas," he shouted. "Here he comes!"

A small submarine about the size of a bus was moving through the water toward them. It did not look anywhere near as fast as the shark—but a hundred times more deadly. An array of torpedoes glinted lethally on a rack toward the nose as blinding searchlights scoured the seabed for a sign of the Turtles. They covered their eyes, locked in the glare, as the beams found them. Red lights winked on along the side of each torpedo in turn.

"He's arming the warheads!" said Donatello. "There's no way we can dodge all of them."

Leonardo stayed calm. "Let's meet our fate well, brothers, as Master Splinter would want us to."

Even as they composed themselves, unable to do anything in the face of certain death, they saw a familiar metal-masked face appear at a porthole. At his moment of triumph the Shredder could not resist taking the time to gloat. The Turtles could not see his expression under the mask, but there was no doubt that he was smiling evilly.

Ironically, though, the Shredder's overwhelming hatred of his foes was what saved them. In the seconds that he delayed firing in order to relish his victory, April was lowering the magnet the last few yards toward his submarine. As she switched it on, a shudder ran through the vessel. Then, nose first, it began to rise out of control. The Shredder's face vanished from the porthole.

"Hey, Leo, you can open your eyes," said Raphael. "We're saved!"

Leonardo glared at him, since this time he had had his eyes open all along. "The Shredder won't risk capture on the surface," he said, ignoring Raphael's remark. "Quick—we have to find him before he gets away."

As they swam up after the sub—now caught inescapably by the powerful magnetic field—their beams gave a glimpse of a hatch opening in the side. They momentarily caught sight of a shadowy figure wearing an oxygen tank on his back, then he was lost in the gloom.

"He abandoned ship," said Michaelangelo.

"First time I heard of anyone leaving a *surfacing* ship," said Raphael.

Donatello laughed. "With all the steel armor he wears, the Shredder won't be going anywhere. He'll be pulled right up onto the magnet. We've got him, guys!"

"Or rather, April's got him," said Leonardo. "Let's get up to the *Masefield*."

Reaching the surface, they scrambled

up on deck and rushed over just as April was maneuvering the magnet up out of the water. The Shredder's sub broke the surface and bobbed in the waves alongside the ship. April swung the magnet over the deck and switched it off. A suit of metal armor fell from it, landing with a clang at the Turtle's feet.

"He's lost weight," observed Raphael, as Leonardo lifted the faceplate to reveal . . .

"An empty suit!"

"He tricked us!"

"So he got away after all," said Leonardo with a wry smile. "I must say, I admire his deception skills—but then, he was trained as a ninja by Master Splinter himself."

By this time the entire ship's company had come out to watch what was going on. The Captain came over with Dr. Gascoigne. "I say," he muttered, bending to pick up something from the deck, "what's this?"

It was another metal fragment that the magnet had happened to pick up when April deflected the Shredder's sub. It appeared to be a torn section of a metal sheet—perhaps once ruptured by an explosive shell, to judge from the ragged and twisted edges. Like the earlier objects that had been brought up, it was badly rusted. All the same, a word could be made out faintly along part of it: B-I-S-M-A-R-

"The *Bismarck*!" gasped April. "It was a battleship that was sunk in the Atlantic during World War II."

Dr. Gascoigne clapped her hand to her forehead. "Then those weapons and things we've been finding haven't anything to do with the sunken city—they're only fifty years old, not four thousand!"

"I *thought* it was a bit odd that the cannon had a bore of exactly fifteen inches," Donatello said. "It didn't quite hit me at the time, but what's the chance of that happening if the people who made it didn't measure things in inches?"

"So the Shredder went to all that trouble for nothing," said Michaelangelo. "There weren't any superweapons to be had, just antiquated, old Second World War stuff. I'm afraid you won't be salvaging any of the radical gadgets you were hoping for, doctor."

Dr. Gascoigne gave a shrug and a smile. "I've still got the ruins of Atlantis to take a look at. And considering who would have got his hands on those 'radical gadgets' if they'd existed, I don't think I really mind! Anyway, it's all thanks to you guys."

"Hey," said Raphael, as everyone groaned. "We're not *fishing* for compliments."

Bestselling books by